ECHOES OF THE MYSTICS

BOOK 1 - APOLOGIES OF THE ANCIENT WORLD

RAMAN C IYER

ISBN 978-93-5458-234-9
© RAMAN C IYER 2021
Published in India 2021 by Pencil

A brand of

One Point Six Technologies Pvt. Ltd.
123, Building J2, Shram Seva Premises,
Wadala Truck Terminal, Wadala (E)
Mumbai 400037, Maharashtra, INDIA
E connect@thepencilapp.com
W www.thepencilapp.com

Author biography

ABOUT THE AUTHOR

Raman Iyer is now a musician-storyteller, was an advertising professional but has always been a passionate hunter for stories. A student of Samskritam, he has been initiated into the study of the Vedas, the Upanishads, The Puranas and the Kavyas from an early age.

Going deep into the past and digging out stories and comparing them with a worldview garnered from his advertising days and then as a musician who travels across the world led into these stories and perspectives.

Apologies of the Ancient World is his first book, under the series Echoes of the Mystics.

CONTENTS

Acknowledgements

GRATITUDE

To my mother Late. Ms. KP Renuka, my Grandfather Mr. KK Parasurama Shastry and my Uncle Mr. KP Krishna Kumar for giving me a world of ancient stories to grow up in.

To my Alma Mater Sri Ramakrishna Vidyashala for the privilege of being around Sadhus, interacting with them closely, and taking in the finer details of complex philosophies at a very early age.

To my Samskritam teachers - Vidwan Shri. NN Chandrashekhar Bhat and Shri. MS Kumaraswamy for making me fall in love with the language.

To Shabnam Virmani, Vipul Rikhi and Linda Hess for assuring me that the world of mystics isn't only for the chosen few, but in fact, a beautiful, warm and welcoming space for those who choose to enter.

To my English teachers - Sri. Rahul S Kini and Sri. Arun K Kuthnikar, for literature and perspectives that went way beyond the textbook.

To my Gurus in the Advertising World - Mr.Arun Subbian, Ms. Shormistha Mukherjee and Mr.Suhas Parab for the several ear twists and occasional pats on the back, wrenching out the writer in me, making me capable of crafting my thoughts into words.

To Roshni Devi for tolerating my idiosyncrasies, erratic schedules and being the sharpest critic and a ruthless devil's advocate for all my ideas. She has also very patiently edited this book.

To Priya Brahmbhatt for designing a beautiful cover.
And to Pari, Momo and Kitappa for very kindly adopting me.

Introduction

Life was good, until the age of 7.

Till then I never knew what it was to be admonished, let alone being punished. Being the only "son" in a Brahmin family, all I had known was love and appreciation. Whatever I said or did, no matter how silly or incorrect - be it sloppily trying to walk, or blabbering a shloka, a mantra or a nursery rhyme - was met with resounding applause from family and guests. When I fell down and hurt myself, my mother would beat and scold the ground, but would never tell me it was my fault that I walked incorrectly.

Even the teachers did not raise their voice or rulers and encouraged students through tremendous levels of optimism. Almost every child in class got a 'Very Good!' written in the coveted Red Pen of the teacher for every assignment or test.

I would come back home from school with great enthusiasm. The entire family would be in the living room - my daily live audience as I flung my shoes and socks in every direction and sat on my little throne, handing over my lunch box to my mother. It was a ritual, where I took them through my day and they would applaud, pull my cheeks and gently coax me to freshen up. After my grand performance, I would wash up and have my Bournvita and fresh hot homemade snacks - vadai or chivda or bhajji. My grandfather would have kept my cricket bat and sports shoes ready. I'd be off to play with my friends after wolfing down the snacks and Bournvita.

Life was good till the age of 7.

One afternoon, I waltzed in from school. I sat on my little throne, flung my shoes, tossed my lunch box to Amma and began my narration of the day.
"....and during lunch time I had egg poriyal (scrambled eggs) today."

There was an eerie silence I had never experienced before. My grandfather's eyes blazed fire and he held on to his wooden chair. My grandmother gasped in horror. My mother came rushing at me, grabbed me by the shoulder and shook me violently.

"Who gave you?" my Grandfather thundered.

"Ja...Jaffer"

That was it. My grandfather stormed out. My grandmother followed suit. My mother stopped shaking me, but gave me a menacing glare. She made sure my grandparents were out of earshot, whispered to me "Why did you tell them?" and rushed out.

I was left all alone for the first time since I appeared on earth. No one was coaxing me to freshen up. There was no whiff of Bournvita or delicious fried snacks. I sat alone wondering what just happened.

The "ande ka funda" advertisement by the National Egg Coordination Committee, a government body, would play regularly on Doordarshan. At that moment, the jingle played in my head. I let it complete, shrugged, and headed to the bathroom when my mother came to me with a towel.

"Here, have a bath."

"But Amma, I have to go and play… I will bathe after coming back."

"No playing today, go have a bath."

Now I was stunned. I tried to protest, but was shoved inside the bathroom.

I took a hurried bath and was immediately whisked away to the Puja Room - the room with pictures, pictures and more pictures of various Gods, Goddesses, and Godmen and Godwomen.

My Grandfather was ready and ordered me to sit before him. He performed an elaborate ritual, making me chant every single mantra/shloka **(1)**I knew multiple times. I tapped my temples with my knuckles and did sit ups holding my ears for 108 times, apparently to atone for my sins.

When this was finally done, my mother took me aside.

"Next time you eat eggs or anything from Jaffar or Jason or anybody , don't tell anyone at home."

"But Amma, didn't you tell me to always tell the truth?"

"Yes, tell me the truth always. But not to everyone. Just listen to me, kanna. You will understand later."

I think that was the moment I was initiated into the ways of the world. It entered my subconscious that there is no universal good and bad, and it's only a matter of convenience. My mother made it clear to me that hiding certain things from certain people is the most practical solution for life to proceed smoothly.

Some of us continue to live by the values and codes of conduct instilled in us from childhood - and these are something we have no control over. We don't decide our gender, our families or nationalities. We accept whatever we are given, continue to stand by the values and rules that come with them, and ensure we pass on the same to the next generation. Some of us rebel our way out by totally discarding our conditioning and allowing fresh ideas to shape our lives.

And there are some of us who are in constant flux - a rebel sometimes, and sometimes going back to our conditioned beliefs. But most of us choose to be like my mother.

Convenience before tradition. The everyday battle of survival - managing a household, raising a child while battling inflation, negotiating office politics, relatives, friends, adjusting to the ever changing political climate and recently, dealing with a global pandemic - takes precedence over overtly rebelling and adding to the list of problems.

Echoes of the Mystics is my exploration towards understanding Human Beings as we continue to evolve as validation craving Social Power Seekers while simultaneously exploring an Individualistic Space of Awareness through spiritual quests.

The 7 year old boy is still alive in me. And he still wants to understand what exactly was the problem that day? According to his grandparents, he did something wrong by having eggs. He still doesn't know, were eggs the problem, or was it Jaffar's tiffin box that was the problem?

According to his mother, he did something bad not by actually eating eggs, but by telling people at home that he did.

Thus,

I ate eggs and told people at home. My Grandparents were severely affected. I performed a purificatory ritual, and was made to promise I will never eat eggs again.

Had I eaten eggs but not told people at home, there wouldn't have been any problem. But my conscience would keep telling me that I lied. I might get used to lying and getting away with it.

In which of these two scenarios have I actually committed a sin?

In case A, is my sin nullified by the purificatory ritual?

In case B, would I be punished for two sins - for eating and for lying?

Who defines the Sins? Who defines the punishment? The government, the supreme authority of the laws of the land, was advocating consumption of eggs through heavy advertising. So why was I being punished for abiding by what the government wanted me to do?

> **"Satyam bruyat, priyam bruyat, na bruyat satyam apriyam**
> **Priyam cha nanrutam bruyat, yesha dharma sanatanah"**

> **Tell the truth, tell whatever is pleasant, but never tell an unpleasant truth**
> **Do not tell a pleasant untruth either, - this is the right thing to do, for all eternity**
> - Verse 4.138, Manusmriti **(2)**

Looks like our ancients had figured out the methodology to cheat society's strong impositions!

But was our society always like this? When did we become

so rigid, define gender roles, caste roles and take upon moral custodianship that functions independently from the written laws of the land?

Wait. Before that we need to figure out why we needed written laws of the land in the first place.

Human beings have evolved by rising above every other species on this planet, thanks to a superior intellect, which often manifests as Ego. It's perhaps this inherent nature to be "above" everything that drives us to discriminate, hate and even commit heinous acts against fellow human beings.

Which is why perhaps there is a need for "law enforcement" to remind us, the most "evolved" of all species, that killing each other is a crime that's punishable by law.

It seems to be in our nature to prey upon the weak, to obliterate those who don't belong or subscribe to our "standards of correct living". Had there been no "law" that criminalizes killing, most of us would be doing away with at least 3 individuals in our lifetime!
Anger, passion, greed, lust, envy. These are embedded in our Ego, which is the "Goodha Guna" of human beings.

A Goodha Guna comprises those characteristics in matter that are embedded so deeply in the core, that they become one with the matter itself. These characteristics will never change no matter how much one tries.

It's the Goodha Guna of water to be enemies with fire and to douse it when it comes in contact. Thus, even hot water will douse fire. By inducing more heat to water, hoping it will support combustion, it will only vaporize and disappear, but never be friends with fire.

Powered by the Goodha Guna called Ego, human beings have emerged successfully as the only species to have inflicted so much harm over its own kind.

Had it been left uncontrolled, the human race would have wiped itself off the face of the planet thousands of years ago, without waiting for an ice age, a great deluge or an asteroid armageddon.

This was realized many millennia ago by our ancient masters, who felt the need for an organized society, with rules and laws, punishments and retribution and a strict hierarchy of power that kept individual Egos in check.

It wouldn't be too off-tangent to say that even the 'Fear of God' may have been induced to subjugate the dangerous human Ego.

This is where religion came into play. Humans had mastered fire, stone and metal. They could hunt down lions and tigers, and tame elephants and horses. The only thing humans feared was the wrath of nature. They couldn't control thunderstorms or prevent famines. They were helpless when the rivers and the oceans rose in spate, when the sun beat them down mercilessly during peak summers and when the winds froze them to their bones in winters.

The earliest masters realized this, and thus, personified elements of nature as 'Gods' and set down rules of correct behaviour.
Religion, thus, successfully created a social order. No human being would take orders from another human. The Ego wouldn't allow it. But when these were said to be from the Gods themselves, the fear worked, and human beings agreed to be bound by rules that defined the Good and the Bad.

Religion also cashed in on the fear of the unknown. By offering elaborate explanations to the afterlife, religion made people accountable for their actions. A simple "heaven" and "hell" concept worked wonders. Do Good, and you shall enjoy heaven. Do Bad and hell awaits you. Closer home, it was the theory of reincarnation. No one wanted to be born again in a lowly life form and suffer. It was said that the human form was closest to divinity, and if you do Bad things, you will be demoted.

Hence, the idea of Merits and Sin - Punya and Paapa - acted as a report card that decided your fate in the afterlife. The God of Death - Yama, has an accountant Chitragupta who keeps a detailed balance sheet of every individual's actions, say the puranas**(3).**

Though this helped in establishing order, human beings did not transform and give up their inherent Goodha Guna. They found ways and means to work around 'God'. The earliest Gods who were direct personifications of nature and natural phenomena were replaced by Gods with human attributes. These Gods had the same passion, anger, envy and jealousy of humans, which made it convenient for human beings to continue exercising their Ego, citing references of these Gods. The "Divine Ego" ended up creating an unfair society. Patriarchy, casteism and classism were not just tolerated, but even held in great esteem for thousands of years, and they continue to exist to this day. The excuse being - Gods lived like this.

Every society devised its own rules. What was acceptable and considered 'Good' in one society was a strict no-no in others, and vice versa. For example, eating meat is a strict taboo in some communities, but no worship is complete without a ceremonial animal sacrifice in some others. And both these societies exist within the same ecosystem.

With such variety in the list of acceptable and non-acceptable behaviour, human beings began looking inward. They relooked at the texts of the ancient masters but channelized it within and realized they are blessed with something called Conscience.

This Conscience, an inner voice that constantly talks to us, often gets drowned out with the clutter of external distractions. Our Conscience seems to be blessed with the ability to let each one of us know what is right and what is wrong, without the need for a "Good or Bad Manual" written by anyone - human or God.

Just like how the Ego is a Goodha Guna - an inseparable, intrinsic part of human beings - so is the Conscience.

Should we reflect in silence upon every action of ours, we will automatically realise whether we have done the right thing or not.

Book 1 in the Echoes of the Mystics Series - Apologies of the Ancient World - explores how human beings over the years dealt with the feeling of knowingly causing harm to someone else. Was it guilt or the fear of sin? Did they worry about justice or did they focus on fixing their report card?

From Socrates to Shankaracharya, you will explore different ideas, opinions and solutions. Apart from the ideas being unique, they also give us a clear timeline of how humans evolved and looked at the idea of Sin with different lenses over the centuries.

I've included tales and parables to illustrate the complexities of the philosophies in a simple manner. I hope you enjoy reading and find time to reflect.

What do you think is the most effective way to manage our guilt?

Write to me. My contact details are at the end of the book.

CONTENTS

1. GUILT - THE TRAUMA OF THE OPPRESSOR

Guilt is independent of retribution/punishment. The moment words escape our lips, or we commit a certain deed, we automatically are made aware by our own conscience whether we have done the right thing or not.

Good and Bad are mostly relative terms, dictated by the fluid nature of society, amendments in the law, and public opinions guided by thought leaders/influencers.

But Right and Wrong are absolute, and our conscience, if we make an effort to listen to it, is always clear about Right and Wrong, irrespective of the fluid ideas of Good and Bad.

When we do something wrong, whether we are punished for it or not, we suffer, often in silence. Especially when our actions cause immense suffering to someone else. We may use loopholes in the system to escape prosecution, but guilt will eventually catch up with us.

The feeling of guilt is compounded with the fear of consequences of Sin. Particularly when one advances in years or has a close shave with death. We realize we have much less time than what it seems. Death seems to approach sooner than later, and that's when a sudden recollection of past deeds, and the stories one hears of what happens in the afterlife to those who have sinned, all come together to wreak havoc in one's mind!

This can be called the Oppressor's Trauma - the feeling of guilt after knowingly causing great suffering to others, compounded with the fear of consequences of Sin as described in various texts.

The ancient world has, in considerable detail, studied, analysed and come up with various solutions to not just cope with guilt, but to ensure we consciously follow a path that reduces possibilities of us doing anything Wrong.

2. THE APOLOGY

Apology is a word we often use as a 'classy' substitute for Sorry. We express regret for our words/actions and place ourselves in a position of lesser power, and hope to bring closure to the argument/situation.

However the root of the word "Apology" conveys the opposite! It stems from the Greek Apologia, which means a speech given in defense. Traced back to 399 BC, The Apologia by Plato is an account of the speech given by Socrates during his trial, defending his actions when accused by the State of Athens. He was tried for not recognizing the Official Gods, inventing new deities and corrupting the youth.

Thus, the Apology of Socrates is an attempt to justify his actions and standing by them and he certainly does not "apologize" in today's sense of the word.

So an 'Apology' meant justification of one's words and actions with an intent to clear one's name from infamy or to prove a point - "What I have said/done may have hurt your sentiments or laws, but it is the truth, and I stand by it. I refuse to stand corrected, or face retribution/be branded as a wrong-doer."

This is what etymologically speaking Apology would mean, each time we apologize to someone!

Technically every defense lawyer should be beginning their statement with "I apologize on behalf of my client!" but that would be the end of the case, as per the current connotation of the word.

3. THE IDEA OF KARMA

As centuries rolled by, with religions gaining power as an agency of social control, the idea of intertwining Guilt with Sin and different methods to absolve oneself from the Sin came to be.

For instance, the Christian Confessions and saying Hail Mary, or the Islamic "Tawba" - which means "to return". Contextually it means 'to retreat from the sinful past and return to the mercy of Allah'. An entire Surah (Chapter) called the At Tawba (Repentance) is dedicated to discuss the act of atonement of one's sins and seeking forgiveness from God in the Quran.

In ancient India the theory of Karma was formulated, and is now used world-wide. Apart from finding a place in the Oxford and the Cambridge dictionaries, Karma is a favourite word to describe our present situation as a direct consequence of our earlier actions.

The popular idea of Karma stems from the Samkhya School of Philosophy. The Samkhyas evolved parallely alongside the Vedic school of thought. While the Vedas looked upwards and sought meaning from the magnificent phenomena of nature, the Samkhyas looked at human existence for what it is, without divine intervention.

The word Samkhya can be etymologically traced to 'numerical' - which in this context would be the "calculated, reason-led, rationalist" approach to the mysteries of life. And it enumerates 25 principles of Truth known as Tattvas.

The Samkhyas are known thus because they list down truths numerically. Even the 3 Gunas of the Sattva, Rajas and Tamas find their first mention in these texts.

Guṇas (qualities/innate tendencies), it states, are the three modes of matter:
Sattva - the guna of goodness, compassion, calmness, and positivity
Rajas - the guna of activity, chaos, passion, and impulsivity
Tamas - the guna of darkness, ignorance, dullness, laziness, lethargy, and negativity.

All matter (Prakṛti), states Samkhya, has these three guṇas but in different proportions. Each Guna is dominant at specific times of day, or at specific phases of our life.

There will be times when we are calm, compassionate and considerate. That's our Sattvik Phase. There will also be times when we are caught up in a frenzy of activity, act impulsively and lose our cool. That's us being Rajasic. And there also are those times when we just sit back and choose lethargy - ordering in junk food and binge watching the weekend away, or we cut loose and party like there is no tomorrow. That's us in our Tamasic element.

The interplay of these Guṇas defines the character of individuals, and determines the progress of life. It's strictly a balance between all three, and not the presence or absence of either of the Gunas, that defines who we are as individuals, say the Samkhyas.

The Samkhya philosophy is mostly atheist, though its tattvas have been widely absorbed in the post-Vedic texts, thus making Karma an integral part of understanding life from a Socio-Religious purview.

The second chapter in the Bhagavad Gita **(4)** is the Samkhya Yoga, where Krishna quotes extensively from the Samkhyas to decode the mysteries of life to the confused warrior Arjuna.

Karma - The Accidental Discriminator

The mystics of the Samkhya school of thought envisioned Karma at very profound levels and arrived at its direct connection with the soul. They describe Karma as a form of a pulsating jelly in every individual's Subtle Body (Sookshma Shareera). For easy understanding, we can call it "DNA OF THE SOUL".

These are transferred from life-to-life. Embedded in these jellies are 'Karmic Seeds' - all our thoughts and actions. In every lifetime, these seeds are released into the Causative bodies (Karana Shareera) i.e. the body which the soul takes in a particular lifetime. The seeds come coded with impulses and tendencies which affect the 3 spheres of life. The Samkhyas break down life into 3 spheres:

Jaati - Family & Profession
Ayus - Health & Longevity
Bhoga - Quality & Enjoyment

The Jaati mentioned in the Samkhyas only denoted one's family and profession. It meant to say the circumstances of your birth were determined by your Karma. This was interpreted hundreds of years later as to look at the working class, economically backward families and those born with disabilities as people who had done bad karma in their past lives. This was used to discriminate and marginalize them, triggering the caste problem. The Samkhyas do not mention discriminating against people because of their Jaati, but only pointed out that you will not be born into a comfortable life if you have more bad Karmic seeds than good.

The selective interpreters who used this theory to discriminate and marginalize failed to realize that discriminating and oppressing counts as bad Karma, and they too will have to pay for this just like the ones being oppressed!

Karma in Shaivism

The deep meditative states which Shiva **(5)**often slips into is a recurring theme in many stories. The root of the word SHIVA is Shava (Corpse) + Jiva (Life). Hence Shiva is in a dormant state, a living corpse. He can only be gently disturbed by Para Shakti, the supreme consciousness.

This state of Shiva is the goal for Shaivaite Sadhus. To withdraw into inaction, and finally dissolve into Para Shakti. They aspire to take the route of Shiva to merge with the Shakti.

This school of thought is called the Shaivaite/Shakta form of worship.

Many Shaivaite Rishis imbibed the 25 principles of the Samkhyas and further expanded them. Shaivism propounded 36 primary principles of truth/Tattvas.

The Tattvas of Shaivism look at Karma as a larger, cosmic building block. Its 36 Tattvas range from Para Shakti - Pure consciousness - to Prithvi Tattva - the rules of the Earth.

The boomerang nature of Karma - what you do comes back to you - is a Shaivaite proposition. The Samkhya idea of Karma is a linear transmission. It's the law of averages, where if you do more good than bad, you will get a good life. But Shaivaite Rishis had a more Newtonian approach. Every action of ours comes back to us as a reaction.

Karma, known as the Niyati Tattva, is seen as some kind of a magnetic energy which is crucial in understanding the "coming back" aspect of Karma, and not just as a one way transmission.

Each karma, or action, generates a vibration, a distinct

oscillation of force (vasana). These vasanas are magnetic conglomerates, but in these magnets, like attracts like.

Acts of love attract love, malice attracts malice. And each action (karma) continues to attract until it gets demagnetized. We can only get 'demagnetized' and free ourselves from the constant boomeranging of Karma by remaining in prolonged states of inactivity. The moment we indulge in any thought, word or deed, the magnet gets to work. Hence Shiva, the living corpse, abstains from thought even, and withdraws into Shunya - a space of emptiness.

Getting one's Karmic Balance Sheet empty is the path to Para Shakti - the supreme consciousness, a state beyond actions and consequences.

The Shaivite Tattvas do not differentiate between Good and Bad Karmas - we will keep receiving/attracting what we give. To liberate ourselves, the method of tapasya/penance was prescribed. Long states of silence, abstinence and inactivity - no thought, no word, no action results in no karma - and eventually we get "demagnetized" and become one with Para Shakti.

The Samkhya Philosophy and its extension in the Shaivaite/Shakta philosophy thus resulted in society wanting to be watchful and mindful of their actions, for the fear of having to endure suffering in the next life.

But it did not describe in detail or enforce what exactly are the actions that gain us good Karma, and what are the ones that would result in bad Karma.

Unlike the Halal and Haram or the Sinner and Saint, the Samkhyas simply said all three Gunas are present in everyone, only the proportions vary. It left the individual conscience to figure out what were the right thoughts, right words and right actions.

4. BRIBING THE GODS - RULES FOR CORRECTING BAD KARMA

The theory of Karma from the Samkhyas paved the way for further texts that started defining the rights and wrongs through codified laws known as 'Smritis'.

What earned you good Karma and what got you bad Karma turned into a matter of socio-political power politics. The elite and the affluent were considered superior because of their Jaati - because they must have accumulated a lot of punya or good deeds in their past life. They became powerful and dictated norms and held considerable control in matters of the State.

Prayaschitta - Correcting Negative Karma

With the Smritis now playing a strong role in governance and being the final authority on what's Right and Wrong, there were also measures devised to ritually correct our Karmic "report card".

Now widely known as Punya and Paapa, various texts define how one can correct/wash away/absolve ourselves of the sins (paapa) accumulated through thought/word/action.

These corrective actions are known as Prayaschitta, which simply means "atonement".

This word makes an appearance in the Rig Veda, but not in the context of washing away sins, but simply as remorse expressed towards an accidental mishap. Attributed to Maharishi Angirasa **(6)**, it states:

Praayo naama tapah proktam chintam nischaya ucchyate,
Taponischayasamyuktam prayaschittam taduchyatey

"Any act that is firmly resolved in one's inner conscience by deep meditation is known as Prayaschitta"

Jaimini was a disciple of Krishna Dwaipayana, known popularly as Veda Vyasa **(7)**, the compiler of the Vedas and the author of The Mahabharata. Jaimini composed a number of verses called the Mimamsasutras. The most widely accepted translation of the word "Mimamsa" is sacred thought or revered thought.

Though the original text of Jaimini's Mimamsasutras is lost, commentaries by various authors exist, the most exhaustive being the Shabara Bhashya by Shabara.

It is here we come across Prayaschitta being applied to daily lives, and not just to correct errors during rituals.

He states there are two types of Prayaschitta. One category of Prayaschitta are those to correct anything ritual-related that emerges from sheer carelessness - like blowing out the sacred fire of the altar, breaking a pot used in rituals etc. The other category of Prayaschitta are atonements for "not doing what one must" or "doing what one must not".

The word is also used in various texts, depending on the socio-political situations of the times, to refer to actions to cleanse one's errors or sins.

The corrective actions prescribed in the Smritis are often completely unrelated to the incident and almost no compensation or justice is offered to the one who is wronged, especially if they are women, or members of the lower castes.

A few examples of Prayaschitta measures as prescribed in the Yagnyavalkya Smriti - Rules laid out by Rishi Yagnyavalkya **(8)**

1. The killer of a cat, or a lizard, or a mongoose, or a toad, shall live on a milk regime for three days in succession, or shall practise a Krichchha Vrata penance in addition thereto. (There are many types of Krichchha Vratas, and they all include fasting and prescribe the bare minimum diet - like grass, cowdung, milk etc - just once a day for the duration of the vrata/penance).

2. The sin of killing an elephant, may be atoned for by making the gift of five blue-coloured cows and a white calf of two years of age to a Brahmana.

3. A gift of a single ox to a Brahmana, will expiate the sin of killing a sheep, or a donkey, or a goat, while in the case of a heron-killing, the animal of gift shall be a healthy calf of three years of age.

4. The sin of tearing or uprooting a plant, or a shrub or a creeper, shall be expiated by mentally repeating a hundred Riks (verses from the Vedas), while a Brahmacharin (a person who has taken the vow of celibacy) going unto a woman and thereby breaking his vow, shall touch a donkey by way of atonement.

5. The sin of eating a diet of honey and meat may be expiated by practising a Krichchha Vrata or any other similar penance.

6. In the death of a messenger in a foreign country, or at his destination, the sender of the message, or the person at whose instance he has been sent, shall practise the three penances from the Krichchha Vratas.

7. An act of disobedience or insubordination to one's preceptor is atoned for winning back his favour by fulfilling whatever condition he sets.

8. The sin which results from doing an injury to one's enemy is expiated by making a gift of paddies to the latter, or by winning his good graces in a friendly and affectionate discourse, after having banished all hostile and uncharitable feelings from the mind.

9. Death is the only atonement for a Brahmana, found guilty of ingratitude, or of repaying good by evil.

10. An utterer of falsehood or indecent language, shall live in perfect continence and practise self-control for a month, passing his time in a solitary place and without asking for food from anybody.

11. A man, going unto his brother's wife without any appointment from her husband, shall practise a Chandrayana penance. (Subsisting on just one meal a day with a morsel of food to the size of a hen's egg. This should be increased by one from the first day of the light fortnight to the day of the full moon, decreasing by the same number each day from the commencement of the dark one to the day of the new moon. This is known as Chandrayana Vrata.)

12. A person, going unto a woman during her period, is purified by taking a draught of ghee at the end of a three days fast.

13. The sin of accepting a gift at the hand of an evil or a dishonest giver, is atoned for by his constantly repeating the Gayatri Mantra, for a month in a cowshed or pasturage, and in perfect mastery over his senses.

14. The sin which originates from one's forsaking and deserting a person, who has asked one's protection, shall be atoned for by reading the Vedas to the best of his ability.

15. A man, who has gone unto a woman in the day time, shall expiate his sin by bathing naked in a pool or a lake.

16. The sin which is incidental to reprimanding one's elders or preceptors, and that which results from using abusive language towards a Brahmana, may be atoned for by regaining their favour, and observing a fast for one day.

17. The circumstances of the guilt, as well as the age, and physical capacity of a sinner, should be taken into consideration in determining the nature of his expiatory rite.

18. Wilful miscarriage of a foetus, and speaking ill of her husband, are the acts which degrade a woman, whose very presence should be shunned from a distance.

19. A person of notorious guilt shall do his penances of atonement at a public place, and in conformity with the injunctions of his preceptor, while an atonement for a sin which has not got any publicity, shall be done in private.

20. A killer of a Brahmana shall fast and recite the "Aghamarshana Shuktam" for three days stand-in water, after which he shall make the gift of a milch cow. Then he shall recite the the verse "Obeisance to Soma," (*namah Somaya cha rudraya cha*, from the Rudra Prashnam) observe a fast on the following day, and cast forty spoons of ghee in the sacrificial fire, while standing in water.

21. A wine-drinker or a stealer of gold shall fast for three days, recite the Mantra sacred to the god Rudra, and cast spoonfuls of ghee in the fire by chanting the Kushmanda Mantra.

22. A sin unwittingly committed by a Brahmana, as well as the one which he is unconscious of, is atoned for by his regularly attending to his daily prayers (Sandhya Vandanam) thrice each day, whereas a sin may be expiated by reciting eleven times the Rudradhyaya.

23. The sin of defiling the bed of one's own preceptor may be expiated by mentally repeating the "Sahasra Shirsha" Mantra (The Purusha Sooktam), whereas a sin of whatsoever denomination may be atoned for by practising Pranayama for a hundred times.

The Journey of a Guilty Conscience

One of the most popular means used as a cleansing ritual even today is visiting holy places, known as Theertha Yatras - pilgrimages. Places having sacred stories, always by the side of water bodies, are said to wash away one's sins. The Ganga and Varanasi are classic examples.

There are three kinds of Theerthas - Sthavara Theertha, Jangama Theertha and Manasa Theertha.

Sthavara - stationary, refers to a site - a city, a particular temple, or a particular water body. We have to undertake a journey to the place, bathe in its holy theertha, and worship at the said temple.

A Jangama Theertha is a guru/priest - a living-breathing-walking holy destination. We seek this person, go wherever s/he is, and much like the Christian Confession, open up to them.

A Manasa Theertha is a journey of transformation undertaken by the mind - a conscious choice to reform.

5. THERAPY OF THE ANCIENT WORLD

I completed my high schooling in a boarding school - Sri Ramakrishna Vidyashala, Mysore. Apart from being a world-class institute with 22 playgrounds, an Olympic-size swimming pool, a full-fledged astronomical observatory, a gymnasium, a well-stacked library and a kitchen that cooked the most fabulous meals, the one thing I am most grateful for is to have spent time with Monks. Back then, of course, I was too young to realise this, but in retrospect, simply being in regular communion with those who have renounced the world played a strong role when I faced life head-on.

One of my favourite Monks, our warden, Swami Atmashraddhanda would spend hours talking to guests on Sundays, one-on-one. Actually, they would do the talking, he would only listen with closed eyes. As notorious boys, we would be sneaking around, stealing the television fuse for stealthy late-night watching or breaking into the kitchen to pick up some chilli powder and salt to go with the guavas we had stolen from the gardens. We'd catch a glimpse of him listening with eyes closed, while the person before him would animatedly go on and on. We couldn't hear anything of course, but the person would sometimes vent in anger, or break into tears, or scribble something furiously. Swamiji would have his eyes closed, opening them now and then to just give a nod to assure them that he was listening. On quite a few occasions, I've noticed tears sliding out of Swamiji's closed eyes.

After such interactions, Swamiji would head into his room, and meditate deeply and intensely, and would be locked in for a couple of hours.

A bunch of us, after dinner every night would gather in Swamiji's room, browsing through his books, asking him stupid questions, or just experiencing the silence. We would spend around 30 minutes 'just chilling' in his room.

At one such post dinner chill session, a friend of mine asked Swamiji

"How can you listen so patiently to people! They just go on and on! Why can't they solve their own problems? You are a monk, you should not be disturbed with worldly affairs, right Swamiji?"

Swamiji replied, "You see, we monks have renounced our lives. We have no family, no obligations, no bonds. Which also means, we are like empty vessels. We don't accumulate anything for our own sake. So people come in and pour out their vulnerabilities. We don't give any advice. Of course, the solution has to be found by the people themselves."

"But then why do they come to you, if you are not offering a solution?"

"Because we don't judge. We don't interrupt. But we internalize everything. We deeply empathize, connect with them and give them an assurance that they are not alone. And as "free" beings who don't have problems of our own, we are so affected by their problems that they feel lighter. They feel there's someone else who is understanding their pain. Which is why after meeting people, I meditate long, allowing their Karmas to become mine, and through my sadhana, purify my soul on their behalf. It's the least I can do as a monk with no problems and lots of time. To give a semblance of faith to people saying now you are free from the burden of Karma, having come to me and disclosed your problems."

It was a complete bouncer for me. With no life experience to back me up, whatever he said just remained a memory, without making an iota of difference. I dug into his bowl of Ravalgaon candies, helped myself to a few, did the customary pranam
"Good night Swamiji" and ran out as usual.

Only later in life, when I lost my mother, underwent heartbreaks, went through financial issues that invariably lead me to introspect, I felt myself in the place of those people who'd come in on Sundays to meet Swamiji. Confiding in a monk, a priest, a qazi or anyone with a strong spiritual aura is indeed an ancient method of therapy.

The Jangama Theertha - a Guru, is an enlightened master who is free from accumulating Karma, says the Skanda Purana. Therefore, Gurus absorb the Karma of the seeker, transferring the Karma to themselves, and by constantly engaging in deep sadhana, keep cleansing and ridding themselves of the absorbed Karma of the seekers.

Apart from absorbing Karma, Gurus, like the Christian priests who take confessions, provided a safe, non-judgemental space for one to speak up and empty their hearts. Seekers could give a voice to their guilty conscience, achieve a sense of closure, and find some peace, and feel lighter. In many ways, this resembled contemporary counselling/therapy.

Depending upon the times and individual Gurus, various means as a corrective action were prescribed. Some Gurus would simply say,
"By confiding in me, you have rid yourself of the Karma. Go in peace, now it's up to me to atone for it."

Some Gurus would prescribe certain rituals, some would advocate community service, and some would give lengthy discourses and have conversations on addressing the root of why such an act occurred in the first place.

So the Guru as a Jangama Theertha - a living-breathing-walking holy destination - played the much needed role of setting one's guilt-laden heart free, and helped the seeker cope with the "Oppressor's Trauma" without the fear of being judged or ridiculed.

This helped people understand themselves better, paving the way for complete transformation.

6. KARMIC CHEAT CODES - The Namasmaranam & the Beginning of Bhakti

The Story of Ajamila

Ajamila lived in the city of Kanya Kubja (believed to be modern day Kannauj, Uttar Pradesh). Born and raised as a Brahmin, he grew up to be a young man following the Vedic way of life and in accordance with the laws of the Smritis.

One day he chanced upon a prostitute, and was consumed by passion to such an extent that he instantly let go of the scriptures and his strict, austere practices. He abandoned his wife, and settled with the prostitute, with no means to support her and the ten children they produced. So he resorted to gambling, highway robbery, stealing and thus spent the reminder of his life committing every possible sin.

He grew old and was lying on his deathbed. All he could think of was his favourite son, the youngest, Narayana.

It was his time to depart, so the Yama-Dhootas - the henchmen of Yama, the God of Death - prepared their ropes to lasso Ajamila's soul and release it into another body to suffer a lifetime filled with misfortune.

Not knowing any of this, Ajamila who could only think of his son, kept yelling "Narayana, Narayana!"

As the Yama-Dhootas prepared to ensnare Ajamila, they were stopped by Vishnu-Dhootas, the attendants of Lord Vishnu, the Supreme Soul **(9)**.

The henchmen of Yama roared angrily, "Who are you to obstruct the order of Dharmaraja, the Lord of Justice?"

The attendants of Lord Vishnu, however, were equally adamant, and replied challengingly, "If you are indeed the attendants of Lord Dharmaraja, then you would be able to tell us the essence of dharma and its signs."

A heated debate began on dharma and adharma, and the effects of acts of merit and demerit. The attendants of Yama recounted Ajamila's previous history, which even by the simplest calculations of accumulated merit and demerit didn't look very promising.
They argued that his unrighteous conduct far outweighed and negated his observances of the Vedas and other scriptures. Also, they argued, the attendants of Lord Vishnu had no right to interfere in the first place, as Ajamila had just been calling his son.

Yet Vishnu's attendants stood firm, and proclaimed, "Whosoever utters the Lord's name, even by accident, calls for protection." Furthermore, they countered, "As a fire consumes fuel, so the Lord's name, whether chanted with or without knowledge of the greatness of the name, destroys the unrighteous elements in a person."

"A powerful medicine, though taken by someone unaware of its properties, is still effective."

The Yama-Dhootas had to concede defeat, and the Vishnu-Dhootas liberated Ajamila's soul from the cycle of birth and death.
Many such stories crept up in different texts with the rise of the post vedic Gods and the sidelining of the Vedic elemental/nature Gods like Indra, Varuna, Surya and Vayu.

Taking the lord's name - Naamasmaranam - caught on, and this led to the decline of the Smritis and their prescribed Prayaschittas.

But the act of simply taking the Lord's name without being mindful of one's actions was questioned by mystics. Kabir **(10)**in the 15th century questions this.

> *Maala Japu na kar tapu, mukh se kahu na raam*
> *Raam humara humein jape re, hum paayo vishram*

Simply taking the name of the Lord externally, without feeling the presence or the connection within, is fruitless, opines Kabir. To give a contemporary metaphor to Kabir's thoughts, it would be like entering a WiFi password outside our house, when the router that powers it, lies within.

Jo paani ke naam ko paani jaane woh naadani hai
Paani Paani rath te rath re pyaasa hi mar jaave

When thirsty if we simply utter the name of water repeatedly, that would be of no use. We have to make an effort to seek water, consume water and allow it to be a part of our system, and only then will it be effective.

Though mystics and rationalists questioned and challenged the Naamasmaranam as an effective means to absolve oneself of the consequences of their actions, it did lead to the rise of the Bhakti movement, which made divinity accessible to everyone and took away the thought that rituals conducted by Brahmins alone reached the Gods.

This lead to Bhajans - a musical approach to divinity, but unlike the story of Ajamila, these meant that by constantly taking the name of the Lord and filling our mind with divine thoughts, we would be compassionate and mindful individuals, hence, we would not be indulging in such thoughts, words or actions that would get us on the wrong side of Karma.

The mystics did not question the validity of the Lord's name but only strengthened it by saying do not resort to simply chanting the name of the Lord, if you are not living by it. They only challenged it as a quick fix solution - where you can live however you wish to, and when it's your time, just call any God's name, and you are all cool.

They advocated taking and immersing oneself in the Lord's name constantly and thus, driving our Karma towards Good. And if you have lived your entire life earning Good Karma, the results will be yours. So the Lord's name, the mystics said, is a helpful and an effective catalyst, but not an instant solution for liberation or a pardon for our Bad Karma.

Kabir again says:

> ***Jap Tap sadhana, Kachu Nahi Lagat***
> ***Kharchit Nahi Ghatari***
> ***Bhajo re Bhaiya, Raam Govind Hari***

Nothing works - prayers, penances, austerities. Just keep taking the name of God, constantly. But back it up with your thoughts, words and actions.

> ***Kashi Gaya Aur Dwarka***
> ***Theerath Shakal Bhar matt phire***
> ***Ghaate ne Kholi Kapat Ki***
> ***Theerath Gaya toh Kya Hua***

> ***Do not flaunt your pilgrimages***
> ***To Kashi and Dwarka***
> ***When your heart is still filled with Malice***
> ***What's the point of visiting these sacred spots?***

7. REBIRTH IN THE SAME LIFETIME

Paschatapa - Beyond Corrective Actions

Paschatapa means to completely transform one's life. A close translation would be penance done after a deed has been committed. Pashchat means afterwards, and Tapa is penance. So contextually it means atonement.

The word Paschatapa connotes the same feeling as the ancient Greek word Metanoia. Meta means after, and noia comes from nous, which means the mind. Metanoia suggests a transformative change of the heart, a spiritual conversion.

Metanoia is also personified as a Goddess - shadowy, cloaked, sorrowful, accompanying Kairos, the God of Opportunity. She is said to sow seeds of regret and inspire repentance for every missed moment. Every time we miss an opportunity to have acted in a good/right manner, Metanoia sows regret and creates a field for transformation.

We continue to notice her several times. On many occasions we end up saying words we do not mean, and end up doing things which we immediately regret. In the case of instant messages we get a chance to quickly delete and take back our words. But in physical conversations or confrontations, phone calls or emails, the feeling when we bite our tongue almost immediately and feel a sharp sense of regret is the Goddess Metanoia sowing the seeds of repentance, the ancient Greeks say.

They say that the feeling of instant regret is just a seed, which we can be cultivated and completely transform from our hearts. That process is called Metania. The Goddess will continue to sow seeds of regret, but it's up to us to cultivate and nurture the seeds into completely transforming ourselves.

Paschatapa or Metanoia also has a strong role in ancient stories to help us achieve clean Karmic Books.

The Story of the Repentant King - A Buddhist Tale

Once there was a King who went on a spate of wars and killed many people.

One day, he suddenly reflected and realized, "I have created so much offensive karma, I will certainly suffer the retribution of hell."

He became fearful, made sincere repentance and resolved to never again create such Bad Karma. He even resolved to uphold the precepts, practice charity, build shelter for the Sangha, and offer food, medicine, clothing and the other necessities of life to the Sangha so that they could focus on their practice without worries.

The King's commanders missed the action of the battlefield and questioned the King, "Your majesty, you previously did a lot of killing and committed many offenses. Do you think that the good deeds you have done recently can truly remedy your previous offences?"

The King immediately ordered one of his ministers to fill a big pot with water and boil it non-stop. He then threw a ring into the boiling pot. He asked his ministers to retrieve the ring. The ministers were alarmed and said, "Please, sentence us to death! If the King wants us to retrieve the ring from the boiling water, it would be like a death sentence."

The King asked them, "Is it true that there is no way to retrieve the ring without being burned to death?"

At that moment, a wise minister said, "You only have to extinguish the fire beneath the pot and pour cold water from above. Then you can retrieve the ring safely."

The King told his ministers, "My previous offences are like adding fire to the pot. Now that I have come to a realization, I have made repentance, I no longer create evil karma, and I cultivate all kinds of good deeds to expel all offensive karma. This is like extinguishing the fire beneath the pot and pouring cold water from above. The ring can easily be taken out."

"The Ring is my soul. By extinguishing the fire of Bad

Karma, and constantly pouring cold water through good deeds, the soul will eventually be ready to be taken out of the pot called this body, and attain liberation," the King concluded.

This story reminds us of the story of Ashoka and his transformation after his war with the Kalingas.

Buddhism is filled with such tales, where complete transformation helps one to recover from Karmic imbalances and attain liberation.

A Buddhist sutra says, "The sea of suffering is boundless and dark; turn your head around and you will see the shore."

"Head" means thought. "Turn your head around" is to change our thoughts. The "shore" is the place of illumination and liberation, in contrast to the darkness of the sea of suffering.

Another example of extinguishing the fire of bad Karma and pouring the cold water of Good Karma can liberate the soul, is the story of Ratnakara.

The Story of Ratnakara

Ratnakara was a hunter and highway robber. He would even resort to killing those who resisted. Every day, he would loot travellers, and kill animals and birds ruthlessly. Thus, he provided for his family and took great care of them. He loved his family dearly, and was prepared to go to any extent to keep them happy and comfortable.

One day, a lone sage crossed his path. The sage had no possessions that were of interest to Ratnakara. Frustrated, he decided to kill the sage. The sage spoke to him calmly and asked him was he aware of the amount of sins he was incurring by leading such a life? A clueless Ratnakara requested to be enlightened on this matter.

After a long discourse, Ratnakara agreed he had been living a sinful existence, but only for the sake of his family. The sage asked Ratnakara to check with his family members whether they would share the consequences of his sins with him. Ratnakara was confident that they would. After all, they loved him and lived off his sins.

His wife and children blatantly refused to accept that they had to share his sins. It was his duty to provide for his family. And the consequences of how he managed to do so belonged solely to him, they said.

Ratnakara underwent a radical change. He gave up his thieving ways and spent the rest of his life wandering the earth, practicing compassion. One day, when he saw a hunter kill a bird which was enjoying a moment of romantic bliss with its partner, he was overcome with grief, and that grief manifested itself as a verse:

Maa Nishada Prathistham Tvamagama Shashvati Samah
Yat Krauncha Mithuna Dekha mavadeeh Kaama Mohitam

O Hunter! You will never know peace for eternity
For killing an innocent bird, which was lost in the
world of love

Moved by this incident, Ratnakara went into such a deep state of meditation, that he was covered by an anthill. When he emerged from it, he composed The Ramayana 11 in the same metre as he expressed his grief.

The Samskrit word for an ant hill is Valmik. Thus, Ratnakara became known as Valmiki. And the Ramayana emerged from his grief and repentance.

Hence, the phrase : "Shokasya Sholokam Agatah" - From Grief (Shoka) was born the verse (Shloka).

Many people question Paschatapa/Metanoia as a means for liberation and feel that one cannot be absolved of their sins by simply turning over a new leaf. They have to suffer the consequences of their past deeds, either in this life or in subsequent ones.

The story of Angulimala throws some light on whether transformation completely acquits us from the consequences of our actions or not.

The Story of Angulimala

Angulimala, a forest brigand who kept the fingers of his victims as souvenirs and wore them as a garland around his neck, was on the lookout for his thousandth victim. He spotted the Buddha walking calmly and ran behind him. But to his surprise, despite the Buddha not making an effort to increase his pace, Angulimala is simply unable to catch up. A bewildered Angulimala called out to the Buddha to stop. The Buddha replied that he had stopped long ago and had found stillness. It's Angulimala who needs to stop. A confused Angulimala asks for an explanation, which is followed by a discourse by the Buddha. Angulimala is laden with guilt and instantly gives up his life as a brigand and enters the Sangha as a monk.

Later, Angulimala comes across a young woman who is suffering from severe labour pains. Angulimala is profoundly moved by this, and understands pain and feels compassion to an extent he did not know when he was a brigand. He goes to the Buddha and asks him what he can do to ease her pain. The Buddha tells Angulimala to go to the woman and say:

"Sister, since I was born, I do not recall that I have ever intentionally deprived a living being of life. By this truth, may you be well and may your infant be well."

An aghast Angulimala points out that it would be untrue for him to say this, to which the Buddha responds with this revised stanza:

"Sister, since I was born with noble birth, I do not recall that I have ever intentionally deprived a living being of life. By this truth, may you be well and may your infant be well."

The Buddha revised the verse to suggest Angulimala's transformation of having become a monk, describing this as a second birth that is a completely different life, from his previous life as a brigand.

After Angulimala makes this "act of truth", the woman safely gives birth to her child. This verse later became one of the protective verses, commonly called the Angulimala Paritta, quite popular in the Theravada form of Buddhism, practised widely in Sri Lanka and other SouthEast Asian countries.

Thus, the metamorphosis of a ruthless brigand into a Patron-Saint of Childbirth is an example of transformation as a way to gain Karmic favours.

However, Angulimala's story then leads into an interesting perspective.

While the reformation of Angulimala may have ensured his status as a saint and even granted him Nirvana **(12)**, he could not escape the consequences of his past actions.

So even after Angulimala became a peaceful monk of the Sangha, there are many who could not forget that he was the one who killed their loved ones. They attacked him with sticks and stones each time he walked around seeking alms. With a bleeding head, torn clothes, and a broken alms bowl, Angulimala managed to return to the monastery.

Angulimala questioned the Buddha whether he really

deserves to take all this, when he could slay his tormentors easily. The Buddha convinced Angulimala to bear his torment and said he is experiencing the fruits of his Karma and it is for his own benefit to suffer consequences right then and settle the Karmic accounts, rather than endure another lifetime of suffering.

According to Buddhist teachings, enlightened disciples cannot create any new Karma, but they may still be subject to the effects of their past deeds. The effects of one's Karma are inevitable and even the Buddha cannot stop them from occurring.

After Angulimala's death, most likely from the constant injuries inflicted upon him by citizens whenever he went on his rounds to collect alms, a discussion arose among the monks about his afterlife.

When the Buddha states that Angulimala has attained Nirvana, this surprises some monks. They wonder how it is possible for someone who killed so many people to still attain enlightenment. The Buddha responds that even after having done much evil, a person still has a possibility to change for the better and attain enlightenment, especially when a person like Angulimala has already paid for his sins by suffering lynching and mob abuse without retaliating.

Paschatapa is not just fixing a particular act of bad Karma with a ritual, but transforming our entire life. By making compassion and actions of Good Karma a habit, Paschatapa is said to help outweigh our demerits and thus enables us to emerge with stronger Karmic scores. But it also comes with a disclaimer - we may not absolve ourselves entirely of our sins. We perhaps have to suffer in this lifetime itself, so let the sufferings we endure not lead us away from the transformation process, says the Buddha.

Whether Paschatapa works for the one repenting, we do not know, but it has led to kind and compassionate rulers, policies and measures for the welfare of people and animals, reduction in battles fought for greed - helping to make the world a slightly better place.

8. UNCONDITIONAL ACCEPTANCE OF GUILT

A few years ago, I was in a coffee shop by myself, reading, writing and reflecting. The silence of a non-rush hour cafe, the aromas of freshly brewed coffee and the wifi-enabled, friendly ambience left me alone comfortably. I let my mind wander across different terrains hoping to latch on to something that can be written down in words or composed as a melody. I had wandered into some distant, beautiful territory when I was hurriedly dragged back with this very unwelcome, irritating interruption -
"Sorry, Sorry, Sorry Yaar! How many times should I say Sorry?"

The voice was earnest, loud, full of passion that when I looked up towards the source, everyone else in the cafe, staff included, were looking at the same scene.

A couple of tables away from where I sat, a young man, probably in his early-twenties, had stood up, with his arms stretched wide awkwardly. A weird cross between a bored umpire signalling a 'Wide' on a humid day 3 of a Test Match, and a very tired Shahrukh Khan posing for the millionth time while inaugurating a salon in some distant first world country.

Everyone in the cafe, and maybe in and around the couple of neighbouring outlets, heard his multiple sorries. Except the one to whom it was intended. His appeal was to a young lady, also in her early-twenties, sitting cross-legged nonchalantly, with her earphones on. She was flipping through a Kindle device, and sipping on her iced tea. She even tapped her feet to the music that only she could hear, thanks to the earphones.

The rest of us in the cafe though, had to listen to the wails and pleas of our young man who interjected a SORRY every three seconds, while changing his pose. From Bored Umpire + Exhausted Shahrukh Khan, he went down on his knees, interlocked his fingers and drew them close to his chest. Had he done this in the beautiful church just down the road, even Christ would have forgiven him. Such was his earnestness. Strangers in the cafe looked at each other and a silent message passed through all of us. From being disturbed by the antics of the boy, there was now a collective sympathy wave for him.

"That girl isn't worth it. She is way too rude, arrogant. He surely deserves to be forgiven. Look at how he is pleading."

The only person not affected by this was the girl herself. She finished her iced tea, called for the cheque, settled it and walked out. The boy hurriedly followed her, stumbling his way out.

Consumed by the collective wave, I brooded over the

incident for the next few minutes, passed my judgement while my coffee turned cold. My verdict -
The girl was a ruthless villain, vain because of her looks, and arrogant because she could easily find someone else. She had no room for tolerance, and could dismiss people with a flick of a finger, and turn totally apathetic towards the emotions, however genuine, of others.

"But of course women are like that - dangerous, vile creatures." I summed up my judgement with a flourish.

The years rolled on. Experiences and reflections continued. As realizations dawned, I relooked at my past opinions, ideas and judgements.

Around 6 years later. Same coffee shop. I sat at the same table where the scene had occurred. Just a few feet away from me, the boy had proclaimed his 'sorry' multiple times. I was sitting in the same spot where the girl had literally seen right through him.

When we seek forgiveness from anyone, we automatically assume to be forgiven. We expect people to let things pass, and tell us it's okay. We want them to either get back with us as before, or arrive at a closure with no ill-feelings attached. The latter is more of a protective measure - to protect our reputation. To ensure the person doesn't go about ruining our name in public.

But in either case, if we are not "forgiven" despite saying sorry, it quickly turns into anger. The other person suddenly becomes a selfish, heartless soul. Forgiveness seems to be a matter of right. "If I say sorry, you should forgive me. If you don't, the fault is yours!"

Whatever be the reason, just because an apology is not accepted, is it right to blame the person for rejecting it? Isn't it up to the one who has been wronged to decide whether or not to accept it? Shouldn't forgiveness be sought from a space of surrender and not claimed as a matter of right?

Kshamapana - Seeking Forgiveness through Surrender

The process of Kshamapana stands out from the rest, because it does not seek to correct individual wrongdoing. It takes on a larger view, accepting that as humans it's impossible to live an entire life filled only with thoughts, words and deeds that earn Good Karma.

This stems from the Jain belief that by forgiving ourselves and seeking forgiveness from everyone, for anything we may have done knowingly or unknowingly, we purify our soul.

Hence, the last day of the Jain annual ritual called Paryushana - (coming together) a strict adherence to the rules of Ahimsa (Non-violence), Satya (Truth), Asteya (Non-stealing), Brahmacharya (Chastity) and Aparigraha (Non-possession) are observed for 5 days, and conclude with the Kshamavani - seeking forgiveness.

On the last day, every member of the Jain community

approaches everyone, irrespective of religion, and begs for forgiveness for all their faults or mistakes, committed either knowingly or unknowingly. On the last day of Paryushan, we receive messages via whatsapp that end with "Micchami Dukkadam".

Micchami Dukkadam is an ancient Prakrit phrase, which means "May all the evil done turn fruitless". And this is achieved only if the receiver of the message wholeheartedly forgives the wrongdoer.

So the power to forgive one's actions lies solely with the victim of such actions, and not in any higher power.

Lord Vardhamana Mahavira, the 24th Jain Tirthankara **(13)**says we should forgive our own soul first. To forgive others is a practical application of this supreme forgiveness. It is the path of spiritual purification.

Mahavira further says: "The one whom you hurt or kill is you. All souls are equal and similar and have the same nature and qualities."

The root of Ahimsa (Non Violence) lies in forgiveness. Anger begets more anger, and forgiveness and love beget more forgiveness and love. Forgiveness benefits both the forgiver and the forgiven.

Hence the tenet of Ahimsa Paramo Dharmah - Non Violence is the Supreme Virtue - led to the 'Live and Let Live' principle.

Through forgiveness and Ahimsa, the Jain beliefs attempted to construct a society of peace, non-violence, compassion and tolerance.

But the ritual of Paryushana and Kshamavani again, is not a quick fix solution. It simply means, despite having stayed true to the principles prescribed, we may have committed certain actions that may have been hurtful. It's a period of reflection, acceptance and seeking forgiveness. Not an instant 5-day plan to correct one's sins!

Adi Shankaracharya **(14)**, one of the foremost proponents of Indian philosophy takes the idea of Kshamapana to a level where there is absolutely no fear of consequences. It's pure acceptance of guilt, and laying it all out in complete surrender. Shankara's Kshamapana does not look at the act as a corrective/purificatory ritual, but simply as a heartfelt acceptance, and ready to face punishment - whether in this life, next life or being condemned to hell.

"Punish me, but forgive me. Do not hold a grudge" is the intent behind Shankara's Kshamapana, as seen through his Kshamapana Stotram **(15)**, which can be called "The Song of a Guilty Conscience".

In his Devi Aparadha Kshamapana Stotram, Shankara says:

Matsamah Paatakii Naasti Paapa-Ghnii Tvatsamaa
Na Hi
Evam Jnyaatvaa Mahaadevi Yathaa-Yogyam Tathaa
Kuru

There is no greater sinner than me,
There's no one greater than you to extinguish my sins
You know this very well, Maha Devi (16),
Please do whatever you deem to be right.

Shankara's Kshamapana Stotram is an act of surrender with great courage. It doesn't come with any promise that reciting this will absolve one of Sins.

He leaves it to the higher power to decide what is to be done, and is prepared to face the consequences. He does hint at a mercy petition, by placing the Devi in this case at a position of power, where she can choose to absolve his sins.

But he leaves the choice to her, and does not claim absolution of sins as a matter of right just because one has followed certain rituals and practices.

At best, Shankara feels, we can make an appeal, like a Presidential Pardon, but the final decision is up to the Supreme Force.

9. AT A GLANCE

1. **Apology** :The Apologia by Plato, describing Socrates' defense represents the need to justify one's actions, clear one's image and escape retribution.

2. **Prayaschitta** :Attempts to correct one's actions through rituals and counter the effects of earning bad Karma.

3. **The Jangama - Theertha** :Seeking a Guru and pouring our heart out makes the Guru accountable for our Karma. This can be viewed as an ancient method of therapy/counselling that provided a safe, non judgemental space to speak up, feel lighter and more capable of reflection and transformation.

4. **Pashchatapa/Manasa-Theertha/Metanoia** :This brings about a complete shift in attitude and leads to a transformation in one's thought, word and deeds. This hopes to create a healthy Karmic Balance Sheet, where at the end of our life, our Good Karma will outweigh all the sins we'd committed before the transformation.

5. **Kshamapana** :This is complete surrender, for all faults committed knowingly and unknowingly. This doesn't rectify individual actions, but collectively views our life, and advocates seeking forgiveness as a habit, to rid oneself of the baggage of guilt.

10. REFERENCES

1. Apologia - Online Etymology Dictionary, Douglas Harper 2016

2. The Samkhyas - Classical Sāṃkhya: An Interpretation of Its History and Meaning, Gerald James Larson (2011), Motilal Banarsidass

3. Karma and the Rig Veda - The Complete Works of Swami Vivekananda - Vol 6 ; Tull, Herman W. (1989) - The Vedic origins of karma: Cosmos as man in ancient Indian myth and ritual. Albany: SUNY Press.

4. Shaivaite Tattvas : Philosophy East & West. Quarterly Journal from the University Press of Hawaii. 1983. ;Kashmir Shaivism, Jagadish Chandra Chatterji (1914) SUNY Press.

5. Prayaschitta - Robert Lingat (1973). The Classical Law of India. University of California Press.; The Garuda Puranam, Dutt, MN, (1908), Society of Resuscitation of Indian Literature, Calcutta

6. Sthavara-Jangama-Manasa-Theertha - Ganesh Vasudeo Tagare (1996) - Studies in Skanda Purāṇa. Motilal Banarsidass ; Krishan Sharma;

Anil Kishore Sinha; Bijon Gopal Banerjee (2009) - Anthropological Dimensions of Pilgrimage. Northern Book Centre; Geoffrey Waring Maw - Pilgrims in Hindu Holy Land: Sacred Shrines of the Indian Himalayas, Sessions Book Trust, 1997

7. The Story of Ajamila - Bhagavata Puranam, Canto VI, Ch 1-2

8. Metanoia - Myers, Kelly A., "Metanoia and the Transformation of Opportunity", Rhetoric Society Quarterly, Vol. 41

9. The Story of the Repentant King - Buddhagate.org

10. The Story of Valmiki - The Skanda Purana, Part 17, (Ancient Indian Tradition and Mythology Series, Vol. LXV), Motilal Banarsidass, 2002.

11. The Story of Angulimala, the Angulimala Paritta and the Satyavachana - Buswell, Robert E. Jr.; Lopez, Donald S. Jr. (2013). "Aṅgulimāla", Princeton Dictionary of Buddhism. Princeton University Press.

12. Kshamavani - Doniger, Wendy, ed. Encyclopedia of World Religions, Merriam-Webster, 1999 ; Chapple. C.K. Jainism and Ecology: Nonviolence in the Web of Life Delhi:Motilal Banarasidas, 2006

13. Devi Aparadha Kshamapana Stotram - Adi Shankara's Works at a Glance - kamakoti.org

11. AFTERWORD

NEXT IN ECHOES OF THE MYSTICS SERIES
BOOK 2: TWEETS OF THE ANCIENT WORLD

The author can be reached on his instagram @ramaniyer
&
via email : echoesofthemystics@gmail.com
www.ramaniyer.in

Glossary

1. **Shlokas & Mantras**: A shloka is a form used extensively in Sanskrit poetry, epics, religious texts and even plays. It is broken either into 4 quarter verses, with 8 syllables each or 2 half-verses, 16 syllables each. This makes it easier to form a quatrain or a couplet - thus, can be committed to memory with less effort, compared to long eloquent passages..

A Mantra is a sacred sound. It can be a single word, or a group of words. They can have a defined syntax and mean something definite, or can be abstract/devoid of literal meaning. The earliest of sacred sounds in India are the chants in the Rig Veda and the Sama Veda. Buddhist Mantras are in the Pali language. The sonic vibrations caused by uttering/listening to the mantras are said to be more powerful than their literal translations.

2. **Manusmriti**: The Manusmriti is an ancient manual of codified laws that once dictated the social, religious, legal and political structure of vast parts of India, and even beyond - Myanmar, Thailand, Indonesia and Cambodia. Some rules from this text continue to influence social norms even today, especially the role of women, whose status in society is supposed to be lower than men, as per the text. Some view this text as barbaric, while some

glorify it. This myopic view of both sides can be justified or argued with, depending on which side of privilege we are.

However, the text in its entirety isn't a linear work, but something that evolved over centuries. It gives us a glimpse of the "rights and wrongs" of an era, and simply documented what was acceptable for those times. It isn't a work of a single author. It evolved over hundreds of years, and the text in its final form was devised between 2nd Century BC to 3 Century AD.

It's called Manusmriti because it's envisioned as a discourse between Swayambhuva Manu - the first man on earth - who passes on his wisdom to Bhrigu - the first teacher on earth to spread his knowledge.

3. **Puranas**: Puranas are stories and legends, ranging from creation-myths to moral standpoints. The major puranas evolved between the 3rd Century AD and 10th Century AD, while the minor ones continued to develop till the 17th century.

Purana simply means "Ancient". Many puranas were commissioned by the victors to promote their patron GOD, and infused their ideals and way of life into the lives of the Gods. For a text to be considered a "Purana" it must have a genesis story (how the world came to be?) , along with meeting several other conditions.

Ancient stories without a creation story are called "itihasas" - history. Hence a collection of "itihasas" is called an Akhyana - an anthology of stories told in the past.

4. **Bhagavad Gita - The Song of God**: The most revered

book among the scriptures of Hinduism, this appears in the Bhishma Parva (The Book of Bhishma) in the Mahabharata - one of the two great epics of India. The Bhagavad Gita is envisioned as a conversation between God (Krishna) and a human warrior (Arjuna) in the middle of the great battle. This text talks in detail about life, materialism, spirituality, duties and also includes several philosophies that are held in high reverence even today.

5. **Shiva**- One of the primary deities of Hinduism, the legends of Shiva are numerous. Though many popular beliefs, stories and rituals arise from the stories in the Puranas, Shiva has a long history, going back to pre-Vedic days. Different legends of deities such as Rudra, Bhairva, Pashupati and many more, syncretised and fused into the popular imagery of Shiva - depicted sometimes as a lone meditator in the mountains, sometimes as a householder with his wife Parvati, children Ganesha and Kartikeya and his vehicle, the divine bull, Nandi.. He is known as the lord of destruction.

6. **Angirasa**- One of the most revered sages in the Rig Veda, the most ancient of all surviving texts in Hinduism, Angirasa composed a number of hymns and also sutras (rules for rituals). He is widely accepted to be the pioneer of the fire-worship (havan), a ritual that's an integral part of Hindu ceremonies even today.

7. **Veda Vyasa**- Krishna Dwaipayana was an ancient sage who compiled and classified the sacred Vedas - the most ancient and sacred texts in Hinduism. He also authored/curated the great epic - The Mahabharata.

The word 'Vyasa' means 'Compiler'. Since Krishna Dwaipayana compiled the Vedas, he is known as 'Veda Vyasa".

8. **Yagnyavalkya Smriti**: Another manual of codified laws that evolved between 3rd Century AD and 5th Century AD right after the Manusmriti (point 2 in the glossary), the Yagnyavakya Smriti addresses Customs and Traditions, Judicial processes and Crime and Punishment.

The Yagnyavalkya Smiriti was comparatively more liberal and lenient than the Manusmriti, so a greater part of Medieval India was dictated by the Yagnyavalkya Smriti which had pushed the Manusmriti into oblivion.

Yagnyavalkya was a sage who is mentioned extensively in the post-Vedic Upanishads and the Puranas, but the Yagnyavalkya Smiriti is composed at least a millennia after his times. The title seems to be a tribute to him, which was the custom in those days, and is definitely not authored by the sage Yagnyavalkya.

9. **Vishnu**: Another primary deity of Hinduism, Vishnu is known as the God who preserves life on earth. He is most known for his Avataras (incarnations) where he comes down to earth in different forms to destroy evil forces that wreak havoc on earth.

10. **Kabir**: A 15th-century Mystic, Kabir was an illiterate weaver who spoke against the misinterpretation of sacred texts and the divisive politics played by religion. He called out both the Hindus and the Muslims for their mindless, myopic views on their respective religions. Though he faced strong criticism from both sides, eventually he

became highly revered by both Hindus and Muslims. Both religions continue to respect him even today. Most popularly known for his dohas (couplets), Kabir made complex philosophies simple, and took divinity and sacred thought out of the monopoly of the orthodox upper castes, and made it accessible for the lower classes. He is also highly revered by the Sikhs. Around 500 of his verses are included in the Guru Granth Sahib, the holy book of the Sikhs.

11. **Ramayana**: One of the two major epics in Sanskrit literature, The Ramayana tells the story of Rama, an avatara of Vishnu (point 9, glossary). The story chronicles his trials, tribulations and ends with an eventual triumph of good over evil. And amidst this, contains many stories with moral and spiritual values of those times.

12. **Nirvana**: The ultimate spiritual goal in Buddhism, Nirvana corresponds to a state of eternal liberation - free from the cycle of life-death-rebirth. This is congruent to the Hindu term 'Moksha', which is to merge eternally with the divine and remain totally free from the pangs of human existence.

13. **Mahavira**: The 24th Tirthankara (Spiritual Saviour) of the Jains,
Lord Vardhamana Mahavira advocated Ahimsa - non-violence, and was largely responsible for Jainism becoming a religion of peace, during a time when conflict was all around the subcontinent. (6th Century BC)
Bhadrabahu, a disciple of Mahavira was instrumental in the transformation of the famous, self-made Mauryan King -

Chandragupta Maurya who had devoted his life to war, violence and politics.

Influenced by the teachings of Mahavira, he renounced his material life and retired to the hills of Shravanabelagola, in present day Karnataka, South India. The hills are still known as Chandragiri, after Chandragupta Maurya.

14. **Adi Shankaracharya**: A scholar, philosopher and a saint, Adi Shankaracharya wrote extensive commentaries on several Hindu Scriptures apart from composing several hymns. He propounded the Advaita philosophy - the presence of the divine within every individual soul and also established four mathas (Monasteries) across the country. Known as Shankara Mathas, these four still exist, following a long tradition unbroken across centuries. The chief pontiff of each Monastery assumes the title "Shankaracharya", hence many works attributed to 'Shankaracharya" may have well been written by others. The original founder is always referred to as Adi Shankaracharya.

15. **Stotrams**: Stotrams or Stotras in the Sanskrit Language are meant to be a eulogy - hymns of praise to the divine. These are meant to be melodically sung in devotion. Lyrically they can be a prayer, or a conversation with any deity, or even a simple description of the deity's powers. But they are always poetic, and always sung and rarely recited as a spoken verse.

16. **Maha Devi/Mahadevi**: Another term to describe the divine feminine, the greatest of all - humans and gods. Devi refers to a goddess and Maha refers to "great". So

Mahadevi is the greatest Goddess, the supreme force in the universe, encompassing all Gods, Goddesses, Planets and Celestial Bodies.

The Devi was one of the earliest worshipped deities in ancient India. Archaeological evidence suggests the worship of a "devi" thousands of years before even the Rig Vedic Era. (1500 BC - 1000 BC)

The earliest evidence of what appears to be a shrine for the Goddess was discovered in Baghor, Sidhi district, Madhya Pradesh. The excavations, carried out under the guidance of noted archaeologist G. R. Sharma of Allahabad University and J. Desmond Clark of the University of California and assisted by Jonathan Mark Kenoyer and J.N. Pal, dated the site between 9000 B.C and 8000 B.C.

9 789354 582349